The Murder of Henry Clerval

The Murder of Henry Clerval
A Lost Chapter to Mary Shelley's
Frankenstein

Story and Cover Photos
By
Richard Hassler

Copyright 2015.

PREFACE

During my undergraduate days in college, the professor of an 11-week English course I was taking assigned the Mary Shelley classic *Frankenstein* as the only required novel for the class. Apart from exposing us to Shelley's vocabulary and writing style, our professor used *Frankenstein* as a way for us to understand how Hollywood twists popular classic literature. However, this professor went a step further. With his love of logic and metaphor, he would quiz us weekly about vocabulary, specific details, and apparent inconsistencies in Shelley's writing. He wanted us to understand the complete storyline, including the agreement of days, dates, and events. Around week 7, he presented the class with an interesting question about an episode in the book.

"Consider the character Henry Clerval." He said. "Spoiler alert if you haven't read chapter 21 yet … but … Clerval is murdered."

I had already finished the book, so this came as no surprise to me.

"So what are the circumstances surrounding his murder" the professor asked the class.

At first, there was nothing but silence. Then a student spoke up and said, "We don't know, do we? That is, Shelley doesn't tell us. Right?"

"You are correct" the professor replied. "But I always thought it would be interesting for someone to write an additional chapter to *Frankenstein* that address this missing detail."

After class, I asked the professor if I could accept his challenge and draft my missing chapter explaining Clerval's murder. I would do this as the final written assignment for our course. He agreed.

I had just over three weeks to organize, plan, draft, edit, review, revise, check, and finish my literary short story "The Murder of Henry Clerval." At 2000 to 4000 words (the typical word count range for a chapter in *Frankenstein*), this proved to be no easy task of concise discourse. My account of Clerval's murder had to tie together dozens of facts, including a timeline consistent with events in the surrounding chapters. I also needed to copy Shelley's writing style and include metaphors of similar depth and type.

I finished my story the evening before the last day of class. When I submitted it the following morning, the professor commented that he was looking forward to reading it. I recall meeting with him during his office hours a few days later to receive a handshake and a grade of 'A' on "*The Murder of Henry Clerval.*" The professor then suggested I enroll in an upcoming Honors English course (taught by a different professor) and that he would be happy to write a letter of recommendation for me. He did, I was accepted into Honors English, and my college career continued. Although this addendum chapter to Mary Shelley's classic went into my coursework archive, it never left my mind. Now two decades later, "The Murder of Henry Clerval" is available for all to consider.

Richard Hassler

Prologue

To understand The Murder of Henry Clerval, it is important to first appreciate specific aspects of Mary Shelley's original masterpiece <u>Frankenstein</u> away from its Hollywood influences. One cannot fully grasp Clerval's murder without becoming familiar with the structure and form of Shelley's book, the main story and characters, a few metaphors, and some basic geography and timing. This prologue sets the stage for Clerval's murder, which is essential for those who have not read <u>Frankenstein</u>.

The form of Mary Shelley *Frankenstein* is layered and complex. The story is actually told by an English explorer, Captain Walton, in a series of letters to his sister, Mrs. Saville. Walton rescues Victor Frankenstein from an ice shelf during Walton's sea voyage north. Victor then narrates his story to Walton aboard ship in chapters 1 through 10 and 17 through the beginning of 24. In chapters 11 through 16, Victor also recounts to Walton the creature's story in first-person, just as the creature had narrated it to him previously. Chapter 24 begins with the conclusion of Victor's narration to Walton, then Walton's letters continue. Walton writes of Victor's death aboard ship followed shortly thereafter by the appearance of the creature beside Victor's corpse. While the creature is speaking to Walton, he mentions Henry Clerval. This is the point where I end chapter 24. Chapter 25 begins with *The Murder of Henry Clerval*, which is the creature's detailed account to Walton of Clerval's murder.

In chapter 5 we learn of Victor's childhood companion Henry Clerval who fulfilled his need for boyhood companionship when Victor otherwise kept largely to himself.

> *"It was my temper to avoid a crowd, and to attach myself fervently to a few. I was indifferent, therefore, to my schoolfellows in general; but I united myself in the bonds of the closest friendship to one among them. Henry Clerval ... was a boy of singular talent and fancy. He loved enterprise, hardship, and even danger, for its own sake."*
> *-Chapter 2*

Victor's early narrations describe the depraved covert assembly of his creature whose living appearance is a massive, disorganized mess of tissue, muscle, and bone not fit for view by man or beast.

> *"His yellow skin scarcely covered the work of muscles and arteries beneath; his hair was of a lustrous black, and flowing; his teeth of a pearly whiteness; but these luxuriances only formed a more horrid contrast with his watery eyes, that seemed almost of the same colour as the dun white sockets in which they were set, his shrivelled complexion and straight black lips."*
> *-Chapter 5*

Disgusted by his now animated creation, Victor quickly vacates his apartment laboratory and the creature escapes. Victor then spends a sleepless night in the courtyard of his residence.

"... I ... rushed down stairs. I took refuge in the courtyard belonging to the house which I inhabited; where I remained during the rest of the night, walking up and down in the greatest agitation, listening attentively, catching and fearing each sound as if it were to announce the approach of the demoniacal corpse to which I had so miserably given life."
-Chapter 5

The following morning, Victor encounters Henry Clerval, which lightens his mood as they walk back toward Victor's apartment. Victor finds the apartment empty and Clerval suspects nothing.

"Entreating him [Clerval], therefore, to remain a few minutes at the bottom of the stairs, I darted up towards my own room ... I then paused ... threw the door forcibly open ... but nothing appeared ... the apartment was empty."
-Chapter 5

Later, in a letter from Victor's father, we learn that Victor's brother William is murdered.

"William is dead!--that sweet child, whose smiles delighted and warmed my heart, who was so gentle, yet so gay! Victor, he is murdered."
-Chapter 7

This murder results in the false conviction and tragic execution of Victor's childhood companion, a servant named Justine, who had been framed for William's death by the creature.

"Justine Moritz! Poor, poor girl, is she the accused? But it is wrongfully; every one knows that; no one believes it ... The ballots had been thrown; they were all black, and Justine was condemned ... And on the morrow Justine died ... She perished on the scaffold as a murderess."
-Chapters 7 and 8

Later in the story, while trying to remove himself from the tragic events that thus far had destroyed his life, Victor encounters his creation on a glacier near Mont Blanc and considers a fight to the death.

"I perceived, as the shape came nearer (sight tremendous and abhorred!) that it was the wretch whom I had created. I trembled with rage and horror, resolving to wait his approach, and then close with him in mortal combat."
-Chapter 10

The creature evades Victor's advance and convinces him to listen to his story. Victor reluctantly agrees.

"My rage was without bounds; I sprang on him, impelled by all the feelings which can arm one being against the existence of another. He easily eluded me, and said--"Be calm! I entreat you to hear me, before you give vent to your hatred on my devoted head." But I consented to listen; and, seating myself by the fire which my odious companion had lighted, he thus began his tale."
-Chapter 10

During the creature's 6-chapter narrative, we learn of his benevolent ways, yet he is continuously rejected because of his repulsive appearance.

> *"He* [an old man in a hut] *turned on hearing a noise; and, perceiving me, shrieked loudly, and, quitting the hut, ran across the fields with a speed of which his debilitated form hardly appeared capable."*
> -Chapter 11

> *"… but I had hardly placed my foot within the door, before the children shrieked, and one of the women fainted. The whole village was mused; some fled, some attacked me, until, grievously bruised by stones and many other kinds of missile weapons, I escaped to the open country …"*
> -Chapter 11

> *"At that instant the cottage door was opened … Who can describe their horror and consternation on beholding me? Agatha fainted; and Safie, unable to attend to her friend, rushed out of the cottage. Felix darted forward, and with supernatural force tore me from his father* [blind man DeLacey], *to whose knees I clung: in a transport of fury, he dashed me to the ground and struck me violently with a stick. I could have torn him limb from limb, as the lion rends the antelope. But my heart sunk within me as with bitter sickness, and I refrained. I saw him on the point of repeating his blow, when, overcome by pain and anguish, I quitted the cottage …"*
> -Chapter 15

"On seeing me, he darted towards me, and tearing the girl from my arms, hastened towards the deeper parts of the wood. I followed speedily, I hardly knew why; but when the man saw me draw near, he aimed a gun, which he carried, at my body, and fired."
-Chapter 16

"As soon as he [William, Victor's young brother] *beheld my form, he placed his hands before his eyes and uttered a shrill scream ... He struggled violently. `Let me go,' he cried; `monster! ugly wretch! you wish to eat me, and tear me to pieces--You are an ogre--Let me go, or I will tell my papa ... Hideous monster! let me go ... The child still struggled, and loaded me with epithets which carried despair to my heart.*
-Chapter 16

As the creature's narration ends, he asks Victor to construct for him a female companion of similar stature and appearance, which the creature promises will end his rampage against all humanity.

"I am alone, and miserable; man will not associate with me; but one as deformed and horrible as myself would not deny herself to me. My companion must be of the same species, and have the same defects. This being you must create." ... *"If you consent, neither you nor any other human being shall ever see us again: I will go to the vast wilds of South America. My food is not that of man; I do not destroy the*

lamb and the kid to glut my appetite; acorns and berries afford me sufficient nourishment."
-Chapters 16 & 17

The creature's tragic story moves Victor, perhaps through guilt, and he agrees to the creature's demands.

> *"After a long pause of reflection, I concluded that the justice due both to him and my fellow-creatures demanded of me that I should comply with his request. Turning to him, therefore, I said--"I consent to your demand, on your solemn oath to quit Europe for ever, and every other place in the neighbourhood of man, as soon as I shall deliver into your hands a female who will accompany you in your exile."*
> *-Chapter 17*

As they separate, the creature tells Victor that he will watch his progress and appear when he is finished.

> *"Depart to your home, and commence your labours: I shall watch their progress with unutterable anxiety; and fear not but that when you are ready I shall appear."*
> *-Chapter 17*

There are many good reasons for Victor to construct the creature's female companion in solitude, far away from his home, friends, and family in Geneva.

> *"... I had an insurmountable aversion to the idea of engaging myself in my loathsome task in my father's house, while in habits of familiar intercourse with those I loved. I knew that a*

> *thousand fearful accidents might occur, the*
> *slightest of which would disclose a tale to thrill*
> *all connected with me with horror ... I must*
> *absent myself from all I loved while thus*
> *employed."*
> *-Chapter 18*

Victor chooses England to prepare for his project. But, understanding Victor's need for companionship, his father and Elizabeth (Victor's fiancée) arrange for Henry Clerval to meet him in-route to England via Strasburgh.

> *"I expressed a wish to visit England; but,*
> *concealing the true reasons of this request, I*
> *clothed my desires under a guise which excited*
> *no suspicion ... One paternal kind precaution*
> *he* [Victor's father] *had taken to ensure my*
> *having a companion. Without previously*
> *communicating with me, he had, in concert with*
> *Elizabeth, arranged that Clerval should join me*
> *at Strasburgh."*
> *-Chapter 18*

Victor and Henry unite in Strasburgh then travel to Rotterdam for their subsequent sea voyage to England.

> *"We had agreed to descend the Rhine River in*
> *a boat from Strasburgh to Rotterdam, whence*
> *we might take shipping for London."*
> *-Chapter 18*

Victor and Henry stay in London for a few months. After accepting an invitation from an acquaintance to travel north, they relocate to Perth in Scotland. This was also convenient for Victor's construction project.

> *"We accordingly determined to commence our journey towards the north at the expiration of another month … I packed up my chemical instruments, and the materials I had collected, resolving to finish my labours in some obscure nook in the northern highlands of Scotland."*
> *-Chapter 19*

Victor needs to get started alone, but he dare not alert Henry to his plan. He must separate from Clerval right away. Henry does not want Victor to leave him, but concedes to his wish. Their separation in Perth is the last time Victor sees Henry alive.

> *"… I was in no mood to laugh and talk with strangers, or enter into their feelings or plans with the good humour expected from a guest; and accordingly I told Clerval that I wished to make the tour of Scotland alone … Henry wished to dissuade me; but, seeing me bent on this plan, ceased to remonstrate."*
> *-Chapter 19*

Victor tours the northern highlands of Scotland and chooses a remote, nearly uninhabited islet in the Orkney Islands to commence construction of the creature's female companion.

> *"Having parted from my friend, I determined to visit some remote spot of Scotland … With this resolution I … fixed on one of the remotest of the Orkneys as the scene of my labours. It was a place fitted for such a work, being hardly more*

than a rock, whose high sides were continually beaten upon by the waves ... On the whole island there were but three miserable huts, and one of these was vacant when I arrived."
-Chapter 19

One night, as he nears completion of the creature's female counterpart, Victor observes the creature watching his progress. Realizing his own madness, Victor dismembers his unfinished female creation as the creature looks on.

"I trembled, and my heart failed within me; when, on looking up, I saw, by the light of the moon, the daemon at the casement. A ghastly grin wrinkled his lips as he gazed on me, where I sat fulfilling the task which he had allotted to me ... As I looked on him, his countenance expressed the utmost extent of malice and treachery. I thought with a sensation of madness on my promise of creating another like to him, and trembling with passion, tore to pieces the thing on which I was engaged. The wretch saw me destroy the creature on whose future existence he depended for happiness, and, with a howl of devilish despair and revenge, withdrew."
-Chapter 20

The creature departs, then returns a few hours later in a small boat and confronts Victor with threats of revenge.

"Several hours passed ... until my ear was suddenly arrested by the paddling of oars near the shore, and a person landed close to my

house ... the door opened, and the wretch whom I dreaded appeared. Shutting the door, he approached me, and said, in a smothered voice--"You have destroyed the work which you began ... but beware! your hours will pass in dread and misery, and soon the bolt will fall which must ravish from you your happiness for ever ... revenge remains--revenge, henceforth dearer than light or food ... Beware; for I am fearless, and therefore powerful. I will watch with the wiliness of a snake, that I may sting with its venom ... I go; but remember, I shall be with you on your wedding-night."
-Chapter 20

The creature quickly leaves again, departing in his boat with almost supernatural speed.

(My account of Clerval's murder begins here chronologically, but as a chapter in the book, it becomes part of chapter 25)

"In a few moments I saw him in his boat, which shot across the waters with an arrowy swiftness, and was soon lost amidst the waves."
-Chapter 20

The creature does not appear again until the wedding night of Victor and Elizabeth.

Victor does not sleep for the rest of the night. Late the following morning, he strolls along the beach and succumbs to his body's need for sleep. Victor remains asleep until late afternoon when he receives some letters, one from Henry Clerval imploring him to return to Perth.

> *"When it became noon, and the sun rose higher, I lay down on the grass, and was overpowered by a deep sleep. I had been awake the whole of the preceding night ... One of the men brought me a packet; it contained letters from Geneva, and one from Clerval, entreating me to join him ... He besought me, therefore, to leave my solitary isle, and to meet him at Perth."*
> *-Chapter 20*

Victor plans to leave the islet in two days, but first must dispose of his dismembered female experiment. He places its remains in a rock-laden basket with the intent of discarding it at sea that night and quickly return to shore. He is successful with the disposal, but he falls asleep in his little boat shortly thereafter.

> *"Between two and three in the morning the moon rose; and I then, putting my basket aboard a little skiff, sailed out about four miles from the shore ... I took advantage of the moment of darkness, and cast my basket into the sea ... and, fixing the rudder in a direct position, stretched myself at the bottom of the boat. Clouds hid the moon, everything was obscure, and I heard only the sound of the boat, as its keel cut through the waves; the murmur lulled me, and in a short time I slept soundly."*
> *-Chapter 20*

Victor awakens late the following morning. He is lost at sea in heavy swells and unable to navigate, so he lets the wind determine his direction and speed.

"... when I awoke I found that the sun had already mounted considerably. The wind was high, and the waves continually threatened the safety of my little skiff ... I endeavoured to change my course, but quickly found that, if I again made the attempt, the boat would be instantly filled with water. Thus situated, my only resource was to drive before the wind."
-Chapter 20

That afternoon, the sea calms, and Victor spies land. He has unknowingly ended up in Ireland. He navigates to a suitable place to dock expecting a warm welcome. He is met, however, with hostility and treated as the prime suspect in the murder of a man found there the night before.

"... as the sun declined towards the horizon, the wind died away into a gentle breeze, and the sea became free from breakers ... when suddenly I saw a line of high land towards the south ... I carefully traced the windings of the land, and hailed a steeple which I at length saw issuing from behind a small promontory ... As I turned the promontory, I perceived a small neat town and a good harbour, which I entered, my heart bounding with joy at my unexpected escape ..."will you be so kind as to tell me the name of this town, and inform me where I am?" "You will know that soon enough," replied a man with a hoarse voice. "May be you are come to a place that will not prove much to your taste; but you will not be consulted as to your quarters, I promise you." ... "surely it is not the custom of Englishmen to receive strangers so

inhospitably." "I do not know," said the man, "what the custom of the English may be; but it is the custom of the Irish to hate villains." ... Is not this a free country?" "Ay, sir, free enough for honest folks. Mr. Kirwin is a magistrate; and you are to give an account of the death of a gentleman who was found murdered here last night."
-Chapter 20

After some interrogation and the deposition of a few witnesses, the magistrate takes Victor to a room where the murdered body lies for internment. Victor sees that it's Henry Clerval and breaks down.

"Mr. Kerwin, on hearing this evidence, desired that I should be taken into the room where the body lay for interment ... I entered the room where the corpse lay, and was led up to the coffin. How can I describe my sensations on beholding it? I feel yet parched with horror, nor can I reflect on that terrible moment without shuddering and agony ... I saw the lifeless form of Henry Clerval stretched before me. I gasped for breath ... The human frame could no longer support the agonies that I endured, and I was carried out of the room in strong convulsions ... A fever succeeded to this. I lay for two months on the point of death."
-Chapter 21

Summary:

Victor's creation is visually repulsive and entirely rejected by civilized humanity. The creature's attempts to gain acceptance and understanding are always met with indignation because he is judged not by his true nature, but by his hideous appearance. Other than becoming a murderer, the creature's solution to a life filled with rejection is for Victor to construct for him a female companion with similar defects, allowing them to live in exile apart from *"the neighbourhood of man."* However, when Victor dismembers the creature's companion before he animates her, the creature takes revenge by murdering Victor's most beloved childhood companion Henry Clerval.

Mary Shelley never reveals the details of Henry Clerval's murder. We only know the cause and manner of his death ... asphyxiation by strangulation at the hands of another, *"He had apparently been strangled; for there was no sign of any violence, except the black mark of fingers on his neck"* (Chapter 21), and that the creature confessed to the murder near the end of the book. *"Think you that the groans of Clerval were music to my ears? ... After the murder of Clerval I* [the creature] *returned to Switzerland."* (Chapter 24) We don't know how it was done, we don't know exactly when it was done (though he had not been dead for very long before he was found), we don't know where it was done, and we can only assume why it was done (we strongly suspect it was the creature's revenge).

For the creature to have murdered Clerval, he needed to row from the rock islet where Victor had dismembered the creature's female companion, find

Clerval in Perth, Scotland, not murder him until only a few hours before the fishermen found his body, "*... on examination, they found that the clothes* [of Clerval] *were not wet, and even that the body was not then cold" (Chapter 21)* and deposit Clerval's corpse on dry land in Ireland, somehow knowing that Victor would end up there the following day. Furthermore, the creature needed to do all of this in about a 20-hour timeframe. Not impossible, considering his near supernatural abilities.

For *The Murder of Henry Clerval* to stand alone as a chapter, it must occur near the end of chapter 24, and be part of the creature's rant to Captain Walton. However, this would stretch chapter 24 well beyond its already expanded length. To accommodate this, the following chapter 24 paragraph would end the chapter:

> *"'And do you dream?' said the damon* [to Walton]; *'Do you think that I was then dead to agony and remorse?' He continued, pointing to the corpse* [of victor]. *'He suffered not in the consummation of the deed--oh! not the ten-thousandth portion of the anguish that was mine during the lingering detail of its execution. A frightful selfishness hurried me on, while my heart was poisoned with remorse. Think you that the groans of Clerval were music to my ears? My heart was fashioned to be susceptible of love and sympathy; and when wrenched by misery to vice and hatred it did not endure the violence of the change without tone such as you cannot even imagine.'*

A new chapter 25 would begin with *The Murder of Henry Clerval* and end with the remaining 9 paragraphs of chapter 24.

The Murder of Henry Clerval

-Creature to Captain Walton:

"You, sir, may conclude that violence comes from me alone, but reflections of his dastardly act upon my unfinished companion cannot compare to any misgivings of which I am guilty. Know certainly it was he who gave me this wretched life, yet failed to honor his promise. Oh, you cannot imagine my restraint as I limited my response to mere threats.

"Filled with anger from my intimidations upon him, he tried to seize me, but I eluded him and bolted from his cottage toward the shore, entirely consumed with wreaking havoc on mankind. My loathsome maker had destroyed my only hope of happiness; dismembering her into a useless mass not fit for the birds of the air or the beasts of the field. I silently yelled, 'Peace and contentment will never be mine. Companionship and joy are for others, but they are not for me to possess. Wretched creature that I am, I will never own a ray of sunshine as long as my useless frame lives.' I did, however, have the power to transform my selfish desperation into action, and so shatter the life of my creator that the toxic fluid of revenge would flow full force through my body of evil. Its bittersweet taste shall become my only pleasure.

"I ran to the beach chased by my anger and quickly reached the shore. Leaping into my skiff, I did not look up through the darkness toward the dwelling of my creator, the author of my despair, lest I became engulfed in even more despondent emotions. I began rowing through the night with furious determination, uncertain of my destination. My course was steered by the direction of the wind, yet at a pace far exceeding its velocity. As a few hours passed, I was thankful only for my supernatural strength. Shortly after sunrise, I spied land in the form of a small promontory, and beyond that, a little town with a populated harbour. The morning sun awakened in me an insatiable thirst, so I carefully navigated my craft toward a creek only a few miles down from the harbour. This remote stretch of beach would help me avoid contact with the local inhabitants. Nature had heavily endowed this shore with trees, and I quickly found a certain outcropping of wooded land to conceal my little vessel. I tied the skiff to a branch and proceeded to search for nourishment, which came in the form of spring water, acorns, and some small berries, a fare to which I had grown accustomed.

"Rage and rowing had so depleted my energy that even this scant sustenance calmed my desolate soul. Soon, a gentle sea breeze eased my senses while delicately teasing both branch and shrub. My thoughts slowly began to reflect on the few joys that thus far had entered my life. My solitude was short-lived, though. The rhythmic snapping of twigs alerted me to the approach of some locals. I hid behind a decaying stump and listened. One man seemed to be telling another about their surroundings.

"'I agree.' the one said. 'The fishing today should be better than yesterday.'

"'Yea, and still Irish.' replied his taller companion. 'Far better than yonder Scotland.'

"Peering out carefully from behind my termite-infested stump, I noticed the taller man pointing in a direction across the water from where I had concealed my skiff.

"'I'm with ya lad.' he replied. 'Just let those Scots try to steal from our homeland. We'd show 'em how the Irish treat criminals.'

"'For certain. exclaimed the taller one. 'If the magistrate don't hang 'em we'll gut 'em like a fish.'

"'Yea. Safe to say we've got the richest and safest island in the world.'

"When I heard this, I once again felt uncontrollable anger rekindle deep within my being. An island was where I spied my creator treacherously dismember my only hope for happiness, as a lion rips apart its prey. An island, I thought, is a most unhallowed place surrounded by the deep abyss of ocean; alone, a solitary lifeless mass permanently affixed thereunder, yet forever detached from humanity.

"I recalled Scotland as the rendezvous point for my creator and his dear companion Clerval. As soon as I sensed it safe to quit my hiding place, I hastened to my craft and bolted across the water in the direction where the taller one had pointed. If Scotland lay beyond, I'll discharge my revenge on Clerval, that beloved companion of my horrid creator upon his arrival. Clerval certainly would not have departed Perth without the one I so passionately hate. With lightning speed, I raced my boat across the North Channel toward Scotland howling ear-piercing wails of unceasing revenge. I arrived on the shore of a village I later discovered was Saltcoats and heaved my little boat into some brush along the shore. I sprinted inland, motivated by disdainful thoughts of revenge while carelessly bounding through barbed shrubbery that frequently pulled at my clothing. I was able to cover a great distance by late afternoon, which brought about long shadows that distorted the true shapes of my surroundings, reminding me once again of my hideous appearance.

"A careful scan of the landscape confirmed my belief that I had reached Perth, the town where that traitor had last seen his dear friend Clerval. My mind swarmed with different ways I could exploit Clerval for the destruction of my most detestable creator. There would be a no more fitting revenge than for me to arrange the untimely demise of his closest companion. Soon I spied a small building with a supply of decaying refuse along its side. Feeling in need of sustenance, I carefully maneuvered to the pile and began grubbing on that matter which had become the very reflection of my being. Unfortunately, the approach of two men rounding the side of the building cut my meal short. As I slipped behind my decomposing mound, their conversation raised my interest.

"'Yes. Victor Frankenstein' the smaller one said, 'I've written him and sincerely hope he will be coming down very soon from up north.'

"'Well then' his acquaintance replied, 'will you be leaving immediately upon his arrival?'

"'That is my desire. We must return directly to London so I may embark on my journey to India.'

"My view from behind the building was just sufficient to reveal the faces of these two men. The larger I had never seen before, but the smaller was unquestionably Clerval, the confidante of my creator. His childlike complexion and moderate frame awoke memories of the unparalleled hardships I endured while tracking them on their voyage north. Rage quickly found its way to the very core of my being. I should rob him of his life immediately, I thought, and let that wretch of a man who gave me life arrive in Perth to be greeted by the news of his murdered friend. Better yet, I contemplated, I'll abduct him and deliver him alive to the fiend, only to murder him before his lying eyes.

Overcome with the sheer delight of this proposition, I threw my hands together as if to clap, striking the corner of my garbage pile. This caused the decaying mass to shift, which aroused the curiosity of Clerval and his escort. I had nowhere to turn, so I

4

sank down in an attempt to minimize my profile, expecting my efforts to prove futile. Fortunately, the two discounted the disturbance as typical for rat-infested refuge and they continued talking.

"The larger man eventually bade Clerval farewell and headed off around the other side of the structure, leaving the young lad alone in the waning afternoon hours. I wanted to seize this opportunity to capture him at once, but I held back, allowing myself more time to formulate the details of my plan.

"I followed Clerval for a while at a distance as he strolled through the woods. His casual gait suggested he was in no hurry to arrive at his destination. At what I estimated to be about five in the afternoon, he gradually worked his way into a secluded area, and for no obvious reason, retired onto a stump and sat motionless in the shadow-drenched woodlands. From behind a tree I whispered, 'The time is now.'

"My quiet utterance caused the feeble lad to pause in his contemplation and rise up. I immediately sprang toward him with vivid images of my plot swirling in my depraved head. As he looked up, shock and fear struck him into speechlessness. With single-handed ease, I slung him securely across my broad shoulders while covering his quivering mouth with my massive hand. I held him tightly atop my superior frame and, aided by the setting sun, retraced my path back to Saltcoats. From there, I would ardently search the sea for my most hated creator, who no doubt would attempt to dispose of my dismembered loved one alone and in the ocean. I determined it most effective to meet him in open water and carry out my murderous wishes away from other influences.

"My advanced capabilities made the trek back across Scotland a quick task. Thankfully, the little skiff I had so carelessly pitched offshore was exactly where I had left it. Binding Clerval with a rope from my skiff and gagging him with a fragment of cloth from my tattered shirt, I secured him to the bow of my boat facing forward, forcing him to view only that vast emptiness of ocean before him.

"With each powerful stroke of the oars, my curiosity was elevated concerning this friend of the one I hated. I wanted to know his story. I began to think that perhaps he might be the one who would understand my plight? As the moments passed, I resolved to release his mouth allowing him to speak. I did not, however, loosen the rope I had secured around his body, fearing the inevitable abhorrence he would surely feel if allowed to gaze upon my hideous countenance. Carefully, and with apprehension, I removed the ragged cloth from around his mouth. He snapped his head back, took an enormous breath of salty twilight air, and upon exhaling, yelled in a high-pitched voice, 'WHO ARE YOU? WHAT DO YOU WANT WITH ME?'

"'Who I am is of no concern to you. But I know who you are, and I belong to someone you know.'
"The lad slumped forward into a nervous relaxation and continued to speak.

"'I know many, yet none of them own any THING like you. Why have you done to me this unthinkable deed? I have no knowledge of your existence, yet you treat me as if I have wronged you.'

"'Just being the companion of my most abhorred creator makes your very existence as detestable as his. I could end your life here and now in an instant, but that is not my intention. You are indeed ignorant of me and thus possess an impartial quality of understanding.'

"Clerval paused and said, 'You speak of your creator. To whom are you referring?'

"'That useless wretch of a man who gave me life, and then hope, but broke his promise when he ripped them both from me as a vulture tears flesh from its already dead prey.'

"'I know of no such person, nor would I entertain the notion of befriending such a vile creature. Please tell me who this person is and my relation to him.'

"'The tale is long and bitter and perhaps not suitable for . . .'

"Suddenly, having maneuvered his binding loose, Clerval spun around and fixed his eyes on my repulsive countenance, which was made even more horrid by an orange brilliance cast by the setting sun. Then, in a most unnatural voice he exclaimed, 'Oh God ... have mercy on me.' He quickly made an arduous attempt to leap into the water but his foot slipped causing his partially airborne shape to fall unbalanced to the deck of my skiff. This fall rendered him cataleptic, sprawled chest down at my feet. Startled myself, I paused, and with rhythmic sighs of contemplation began to visualize the events that had led me to this spot. With sharp, images flashing in my degenerate head, my soul began an emotional crescendo as evil escalated through my veins. Clerval was like the others and I was certain he would attempt to escape my presence when he awoke, even being surrounded by water. I felt it necessary to again secure him to the bow of my vessel, but much more tightly. This time, however, he would not face the ocean, but rearward, forced to visually consume every detail of my hideous form. I flipped the unconscious lad over, but as I gripped his neck to lift him into place, the feel of his flesh in my gigantic hand blended perfectly with pictures of innocent young William flashing in my mind. My fingers began to flex. As the tightness of my clasp increased, Clerval's consciousness returned and his eyes opened and met mine. With his throat constricted, he could not speak but only groan as his lungs struggled in vain to catch one last breath of life-giving air. Words would scarcely have been able to express the look of disgust he bestowed upon me as his eyes bulged bloodshot and his face turned bright crimson. This expression, however, was quickly replaced with one more peaceful and serene--that unmistakable appearance that accompanies death.

"As I released my grip, his lifeless form collapsed at my feet. Could this be true? Could I have accomplished, yet again, that unthinkable act of destroying that which another had created? 'Yes,' I exclaimed aloud in my own defense. 'My creator has destroyed that which belonged to me. I have destroyed that which was so dear to him.' But the death of this one was insufficient consolation. Indeed more, yes, more I resolved to demand from my treacherous creator before I could accept solitude in my lonely gloom.

"As the sun dipped below the North Channel horizon, I drifted a bit, scheming a plan to take advantage of Clerval's fate, thereby dealing a most devastating blow on the one I hate. Twilight then diverted my attention to the island where I had first landed, and my plan came into full view. To be properly carried out, however, I would need to return to that island, then with equal determination back to the sea to locate my creator.

"Fueled by renewed energy, I furiously searched for the spot where I had previously landed a few miles down from the harbor. Soon I located the small promontory and the wooded creek where I had docked earlier. The evening light also revealed a scattering of fishing boats on the sea. I needed to dispose of my creator's deceased companion in total darkness. I decided to first hide my craft and myself just as I had that morning, and wait for an appropriate time to dump Clerval's lifeless frame in a conspicuous location. At what must have been about ten o'clock, a gusty wind from the north motivated those still fishing on the water to head for shore, and thus toward me. Thankfully, the moon had not yet risen, offering an ideal opportunity for me to place Clerval on the shore, away from the approaching boats and locals. I deposited Clerval's body, and upon hearing voices, I quickly reentered my craft and rowed away.

"I could now focus my efforts on the only remaining task; locating my wretched creator. Navigating irregularity to cover maximum area, I ardently searched the dark sea convinced that my efforts would not be in vain. Then, as if nature became my mysterious ally, the moon began to rise over the lifeless panorama of open water. With increasing moonlight, I seized the opportunity to scan the otherwise featureless ocean landscape. But, in a predictable act of fate, the moonlight also revealed a rapidly increasing level of water in my feeble skiff. Even with my superior abilities, I would not be able to both purge my vessel of water and search for my hated one for very long. Then, just as fear and despair seemed victorious, I noticed at a distance an anomaly on the ocean's surface, and as I rowed closer, my intuitions proved correct. Helpless and asleep in his skiff, there lay the source of all my unhappiness; that murderer who, after such a noble agreement, broke his promise and destroyed the very thing that would have been my instrument of eternal happiness.

"That familiar sense of rage again began to boil within, but I was able to contain it knowing how much better my revenge would taste after I completed my disgraceful plan. The swiftly filling boat now compromised my intention of abducting this wretched man to deliver him to his lifeless friend. The water's relentless pressure against my craft quickly exceeded its seaworthiness. My skiff soon yielded to the ocean's abundance, sank, and quickly disappeared in to the depths of the abyss.

"With nowhere to go, I scrambled aboard my creator's craft certain of his quick awakening and angered by my foiled plan. But he continued to sleep. This was a bittersweet moment. Although I was his master, he was indeed my creator. Torn by my unceasing insistence to destroy him and my endless desire for him to accept me, I resolved to use his seaworthy craft to continue my plan. I rowed for hours as night transitioned to twilight and twilight to late morning, and there I was, still gazing at my creator hatefully with one wretched eye and lovingly with the other. Then unexpectedly, he yelled out from a nightmare, 'be gone, ye of Satan's spawn! No progeny of evil shall ever coerce me to comply!' Instant rage gushed through my being with an intensity I had never experienced. I leaped up full bent on finally extinguishing the hateful life of this lying creature. Doing so, however, caused a heavy imbalance in our little boat, which heaved me to one side with such force that I tumbled into the sea with a loud splash.

"At first, I considered reentering the craft of my still sleeping creator to finish my work, but my dive into the ocean jolted him to consciousness. As he awoke, I decided to stay in the water, low and behind

10

his skiff, grasping its stern by the rudder hinge. Although the wind had now increased with waves to match, it was easy to control the speed and direction of the craft by treading water with my powerful legs. Though tricky at first, this soon became no more difficult than normal swimming, even when challenged by the prevailing conditions of the sea.

"Many hours passed as my hated one blurted occasional expletives. At once he exclaimed, 'Fiend. Your task is already fulfilled.' I answered silently, 'Oh ye of little knowledge, how incorrect you are, for my tasks have only begun.' Slowly the sun approached the horizon and the sea calmed. Under these conditions it was easy to guide this wretch of a man to his ultimate destiny. In the distance, I could now see the small promontory and the area where I had deposited Clerval's body. With thirst no doubt motivating him to reach the closest land, I released my grip. With a great gulp of salty air I quietly sank beneath the glasslike sea. Only when the need to breathe became intolerable did I slowly surface and look about. There on the water was my creator, furiously navigating his craft toward what he certainly believed would be a friendly welcome. Little did he know what a shocking discovery he would make or to what hideous extent his life would dwindle with the murder of his dearest friend, Henry Clerval.